My Dad
Count Bartholomew
Moon

Me!
Isadora Moon

Pink Rabbit

For vampires, fairies and humans everywhere!

And for my own little Honeyblossom,
Celestine Stardust.

OXFORD
UNIVERSITY PRESS

Great Clarendon Street, Oxford OX2 6DP

Oxford University Press is a department of the University of Oxford.
It furthers the University's objective of excellence in research, scholarship, and
education by publishing worldwide. Oxford is a registered trade mark of Oxford
University Press in the UK and in certain other countries

British Library Cataloguing in Publication Data

Data available

ISBN: 978-0-19-275853-8

3 5 7 9 10 8 6 4 2

Printed in Great Britain by Bell and Bain Ltd, Glasgow

Paper used in the production of this book is a natural,
recyclable product made from wood grown in sustainable forests.
The manufacturing process conforms to the environmental
regulations of the country of origin.

MIX
Paper from
responsible sources
FSC
www.fsc.org   FSC® C007785

ISADORA MOON

Goes on a School Trip

Harriet Muncaster

OXFORD
UNIVERSITY PRESS

Chapter ONE

Isadora Moon, that's me! And this is
Pink Rabbit. He comes everywhere with
me. Even on school trips! I have only
ever been on one school trip before—
we went to the ballet—so I was
very excited when our teacher,
Miss Cherry, announced that we
would be going on another

9

one in a week's time!

'Oh, lovely,' said Mum when I brought the letter home to show her. 'A historic castle museum! That will be interesting. Would you like Dad and me to volunteer again?'

'Erm . . .' I began hesitantly. Mum and Dad had volunteered on my last school trip and it had been fine (mostly) but I am always a little unsure about them offering to help out. The thing is that my Mum is a fairy and my Dad is a vampire (which makes me a vampire fairy, by the way). They are not quite like other parents, and sometimes it can be embarrassing.

'You can,' I said. 'If you really want to. Except Miss Cherry said they only need one volunteer this time. So only one of you can come.'

'Ah,' said Mum, looking slightly disappointed. 'That's a shame. You'd better take your Dad then. You know how much he loves old castles!'

'I do!' agreed Dad, who was jiggling my baby sister Honeyblossom up and down. 'I would love to go!' He whipped a pen out from underneath his cloak and briskly signed the letter.

Dear Parent,

School trip: Historic castle museum
Date: 20th October
Time: 09:00

Please sign to give your child permission to come. We would also be grateful if a parent could volunteer to accompany the class.

Signed: _Count Bartholomew Mars_ ★☽

'I hope I will get to wear one of those fashionable hi-vis jackets again,' he said. 'It was a very striking look.'

'Yes,' agreed Mum. 'You did look handsome in it. They were lovely and bright, weren't they? I believe the word for that is "fluorescent".'

'Fluorescent!' said Dad. 'I love that word!' He handed the letter back to me. 'I can't wait for the trip!' he exclaimed. 'I just adore old castles. Do you think it will be haunted? I do hope so!'

'I don't know,' I replied. 'I'll have to ask Miss Cherry.'

'Haunted?!' said Miss Cherry in surprise when I asked her the question the next day at school. 'Of course the castle won't be haunted! You mustn't be frightened of that!'

'I'm not frightened,' I said. 'I just—'

'Haunted?' asked my friend Zoe from behind me. 'Did you say the castle was haunted, Isadora?'

'No, I was just —'

'It's haunted!' cried Zoe loudly,
putting her hand over her mouth in shock.

'Oh my goodness!'

'Eek!' cried Samantha, wide-eyed.

'I'm scared of ghosts!'

'Everyone's scared of ghosts!'

said Bruno.

'The castle is haunted!' shouted Jasper.

Soon the whole class was in an uproar. Samantha's face had gone very white.

'Now, calm down, everyone,' said Miss Cherry loudly. 'The castle is NOT haunted.'

'But what if it is?' squeaked Samantha.

'It's NOT,' sighed Miss Cherry, rolling her eyes.

But no one was listening. The idea that the castle was haunted had firmly planted itself into everyone's head.

'I bet the ghost trails round the castle corridors, wailing and moaning,' said Zoe.

'I bet it has red, glowing eyes and very sharp teeth,' shivered Sashi.

'I bet it eats children for breakfast,' said Bruno.

'Oh help!' gulped Samantha, trembling.

'Now, Dad,' I said, the night before the school trip. 'I know you're a vampire, but you must make sure you don't oversleep tomorrow. We have to be at school at nine o'clock to catch the coach.'

'A coach!' said Dad. 'How exciting! I have never been on one of those before.

And don't worry, Isadora,
I will make sure I am
ready. I am planning to set five
extremely loud alarms. The first one
will go off at 5 a.m. That will give me about
two and a half hours to do my hair. It's not
much, I know, but it will have to do.'

'Great!' I said happily. 'Thanks, Dad.'

'Oh my,' said Mum. 'Five alarms!
I shall have to magic up some special
earplugs for myself tonight!'

'Don't worry, Mum,' I said. 'You can
sleep in my room tonight. We can set up
the camp bed! Maybe we could even roast
marshmallows like we did when we went
camping!'

Mum laughed. 'That's very sweet of you, Isadora,' she said. 'But I don't mind really. It's nice to be awake at the crack of dawn sometimes. Nature is very beautiful at that time.'

'Oh, OK,' I said, feeling slightly disappointed. 'Could we still have marshmallows, though? We could have them for pudding tonight!'

'Great idea!' said Mum, glancing out of the window at the wet weather. 'I do so love being out in the fresh sparkling rain!'

'Erm . . .' began Dad.

'I'll magic us up a shelter,' said Mum. 'That way the campfire won't go out.'

Dad looked a bit worried. He hates the rain because it messes up his perfectly groomed vampire hair.

'Maybe we could cook the marshmallows indoors?' he suggested. 'Over the stove?'

'Oh no!' said Mum, horrified. 'Why would we want to miss this glorious weather?'

Dad and I stared out of the window at the darkening grey sky, as Mum pottered about getting things ready for the campfire. Rain was pouring down in sheets.

'I do hope it will clear up for the trip tomorrow,' said Dad. 'Otherwise we're going to get very wet.'

'I'm sure it will,' said Mum confidently. 'It's probably just a little shower.'

But we had to have our marshmallows under the magical shelter,

and by the time we all went to bed, the
rain was still hammering down on the roof
of our house.

Chapter TWO

When I woke up in the morning it looked
even greyer than it had the night before.

'Oh dear,' I said to Pink Rabbit as I
hopped out of bed. 'I think we're going to
need raincoats today!'

Pink Rabbit shivered and looked a bit
worried. He hates getting wet because he
is made of stuffing. I opened my wardrobe

door and pulled out his little plastic
rain cape.

'You'll be fine if you wear this,' I said,
putting it on him. 'You'll stay perfectly
dry! And it looks very smart.'

Pink Rabbit looked pleased. He bounced up and down in front of the mirror, posing and preening while I put on my own clothes. Then we both made our way downstairs to the kitchen.

Dad was already there,

drinking his red juice.

His hair looked perfectly

sleek and vampire-y, and he was

wearing his best black waterproof cape.

'I told you I would be ready,' he yawned,

hurriedly putting on his sunglasses to hide

the dark rings under his eyes.

'Well done, Dad!' I said, sitting down

at the table and reaching for a piece of

toast.

'I'm not too sure about the weather

though,' continued Dad, glancing

anxiously out of the window. 'It's

pouring! I hate getting my hair messed

up in the rain.'

I looked at the black clouds outside and at the raindrops running in streaks down the window.

'We will have to take umbrellas,' I said.

'Ah, yes!' said Dad, suddenly cheering up. 'I can use my new, fancy black one with the pointed top!'

'And I can use my one with the bat ears!' I said excitedly.

After breakfast we went into the hall and put on our waterproof boots. Dad grabbed his umbrella and I put on my pink plastic rain cape with the hood.

'We're off!' Dad said, giving Mum a kiss on the cheek.

'Bye, Mum!' I said. 'Bye,
Honeyblossom!'

We stepped out of the house.

'The rain can't touch me!' said Dad
happily, twirling his enormous black
umbrella above his head. 'Don't we look
fashionable!'

Pink Rabbit nodded in agreement
as he splashed along beside me in his
rubber boots.

When we arrived at the school we saw Miss Cherry standing outside on the pavement next to a big coach. She had a clipboard in one hand and an umbrella in the other.

'Ah, Mr Moon!' she said as Dad and I came towards her. 'You're here! Wonderful!' She put her clipboard under her arm and rummaged in her bag for a moment. 'Here you are!' she said, holding out a fluorescent hi-vis jacket. 'You need to put this on. It's for health and safety.'

Dad took the jacket gleefully. 'Oh, goody,' he said. 'I was looking forward to wearing this again. It's very stylish, don't you think?'

'Er . . .' said Miss Cherry. 'If you think so, Mr Moon.'

'I do!' said Dad. 'Honestly, I'm just too stylish for words sometimes. I ought to be careful I don't get snapped up by a modelling agency.'

Miss Cherry coughed awkwardly. 'You can board the coach now,' was all she said.

Dad put his umbrella down in a flurry of raindrops and stepped onto the coach. I followed him, and Pink Rabbit bounced in behind me.

'Isadora!' shouted Zoe from the back seat. 'Come and sit next to me!'

I made my way to the back of the coach and sat down next to Zoe. She was all bundled up in a raincoat with frog eyes on the hood.

'Are you nervous?' she asked as I made myself comfortable and perched Pink Rabbit on my lap.

'Nervous?' I asked. 'What do you mean?'

'About the ghost!' said Samantha,
popping up from a seat in front and
staring at us with wide, frightened eyes.
'You know, the one in the castle!'

'Oh, that,' I said. 'I don't think—'

'It's going to be TERRIFYING,' announced Bruno knowledgeably from a few rows down. 'It's lucky I remembered my ghost-protector spray. He held up a little pink sparkly bottle, which looked suspiciously like perfume, and spritzed a cloud of something sickly sweet into the air.

Oliver wrinkled his nose. 'That smells like perfume,' he said. 'It's the same bottle my Mum uses.'

'It's not perfume,' said Bruno. 'It's ghost-protector spray. Here, let me spray some on you.'

'NO!' shouted Oliver. 'It smells like roses!'

'I'll have some,' said Zoe. 'Spray some on me!'

Bruno leaned over his seat and spritzed his ghost-protector spray all over Zoe. And then Sashi. And then Samantha.

'Do you want some, Isadora?' he asked.

'Yes, please,' I said. I didn't really believe in Bruno's ghost-protector spray but I did want to smell of roses, like my friends.

Just then Miss Cherry stepped up into the coach, with the last remaining pupils following close behind her.

'At last!' she said. 'We are all here! Bruno, sit down, please. Put your seatbelts on, everyone. Let's go!'

There was a clicking and a clacking as we all did as Miss Cherry said and then the coach rumbled into life. Miss Cherry sat down next to Dad and sniffed the air.

'It smells like roses in here,' she remarked, turning to the driver. 'What a lovely air freshener!'

The coach pulled away from the school and I peered out of the window at the shiny road below. It seemed very far away.

'I didn't know coaches were so big!' I said to Zoe.

But Zoe wasn't listening. She was busy talking to Samantha and Sashi about the ghost.

'We need to all stick together,' Sashi was saying. 'That way, if it attacks, we will be safer.'

'Good idea,' said Zoe.

Samantha nodded, her face as white as a sheet. 'Oh dear, oh dear,' she squeaked.

Chapter THREE

By the time we arrived at the castle museum my friends had worked themselves up so much about the ghost that none of them wanted to leave the coach.

'Come on!' said Miss Cherry impatiently. 'What's wrong with you all? There is NO ghost in the museum.'

Dad's head popped up from behind his seat.

'Oh, that's a shame,' he said. 'I do love a good haunted castle.'

Eventually, after much persuading from Miss Cherry, everyone got off the coach, even Samantha. We all stood on the side of the road as the coach pulled away, and stared up at the castle museum in front of us. Huge black towers and turrets loomed up into the grey sky, and thunder and lightning cracked overhead.

'It definitely looks haunted,' said Bruno.

'You're right!' said Dad happily. 'Maybe it is after all!'

Miss Cherry frowned. 'That is not a very helpful comment, Mr Moon,' she whispered. 'The castle is most definitely NOT haunted! Now follow me, everyone.'

We all trailed behind Miss Cherry towards the heavy black castle doors. Just inside the doors was a ticket booth with a man sitting inside it.

OPEN

'Ah,' he said when he saw us. 'You must be the school trip we are expecting today.'

'Indeed we are,' said Miss Cherry. 'We have come for an educational visit.'

'Excellent,' said the man. He handed Miss Cherry a leaflet with a map of the castle on it and gestured towards the entrance to the first room.

'Have fun!' he said.

'I don't want to go in,' whispered Sashi as Miss Cherry hurried us all past the ticket booth and into the first room.

'Me neither,' shivered Samantha. 'This castle feels spooky.'

'It's only spooky because of the weather,' said Miss Cherry as a crash of thunder boomed overhead and a flash of lightning lit up the room. The whole class screamed except for me and Dad and Miss Cherry. I don't mind thunder and lightning. I am half vampire after all.

'Quiet, everyone,' said Miss Cherry, beginning to sound a bit frazzled. 'The thunder and lightning won't hurt you.

Now look at this beautiful historic room!'

We all looked. It was a beautiful
room. The ceiling was midnight black
with silver stars painted on to it and there
were two jewelled thrones sitting in the
middle of the floor. Miss Cherry consulted
the map.

'This is the throne room,' she told us.
'The king and queen of long ago would
have sat in here. And look over there at
all those crowns!'

Miss Cherry led us all towards a big glass case which was full of glittering crowns. There were tall ones and short ones and spiky ones, and all of them were covered in diamonds.

'Wow,' said Dad admiringly. 'They do look swish, don't they?'

'I want to try one on!' said Zoe.

'You can't try these ones on,' said Miss Cherry. 'They're much too precious. But look, there's a dressing-up box just over there. You can try on the costumes the king and queen would have worn in the olden days.'

'I want to be the queen!' cried Zoe as she bolted towards the dressing-up box and rummaged inside it. 'Ooh, look at this beautiful crown!'

'I'll be the king,' said Oliver, taking out a long red cape with a black and white spotted fur trim.

'I want to be something,' said Bruno.
'But there are only two costumes in the box.'

'There should be costumes to try on
in every room,' explained Miss Cherry.
'You will all get a chance to dress up. By
the time we've been through every room
you should all be wearing medieval outfits.
The challenge is to find all the costumes
in the castle!'

'Ooh,' said Dad. 'How thrilling!

'Not for you, I'm afraid,' said Miss Cherry. 'The costumes are all in children's sizes.'

'Oh,' said Dad, seeming disappointed. 'Ah, well. I've got my hi-vis jacket at least!'

We all started to move towards the next room. My friends seemed to have forgotten about the ghost for the time being. They were busy chattering about all the different costumes we might find in the different rooms.

Zoe walked proudly next to me in her jewelled royal dress and glittering crown. 'I wish I could wear this every day!' she said.

Miss Cherry led us out of the throne room and into a long, gloomy corridor where there were flickering candles stuck all along the walls.

'This is my kind of place,' said Dad as thunder cracked overhead again.

'Eek! What's that?' squealed Samantha as lightning lit up the whole corridor for a second, revealing a tall metal figure standing up against the wall.

'That's a suit of armour,' said Miss Cherry. 'Knights used to wear them to go into battle.'

'Cool!' said Bruno.

'Maybe there's a knight outfit somewhere.'
He raced towards the dressing-up box at
the end of the corridor and flung the lid
open.

'TWO suits of armour!' he shouted,
holding up two clinking silver costumes.
'Who wants to be a knight with me?'

'Me!' shouted Jasper.

'Me!' shouted Sashi.

'You can't be a knight—you're a girl, Sashi,' said Bruno.

'I CAN!' said Sashi, snatching the suit before Jasper could get to it, and hurriedly putting it on. 'Girls can be knights too!'

'Very cool,' marvelled Dad. 'Bruno and Sashi do look sleek, don't they? All that shiny gleaming metal. Maybe I should get a metal vampire cape!'

At the end of the corridor there was a flight of steps.

'This leads down into the dungeon,' explained Miss Cherry, looking at her map. 'It's where they used to keep the prisoners.'

'Oh no!' wailed Samantha, biting her fingers nervously. 'That's exactly the kind of place a ghost would be hiding.'

'Marvellous,' exclaimed Dad. 'I'll go first, shall I?' He started to make his way down the steps and Pink Rabbit, Miss Cherry, and I followed him. The rest of the class followed reluctantly.

'Don't forget,' I heard Bruno say. 'You'll be safe if you've got your ghost-protector spray on.'

The dungeon was dark and cold with no windows. Candles flickered on the walls all around us, making shapes loom up in the dim light. Even I gave a little shiver and held on tightly to Pink Rabbit's paw.

'Very atmospheric,' remarked Dad, peering around interestedly. 'This is the kind of effect I am always trying to create in my bathroom. I do so love candlelit baths.'

'Hmm,' said Miss Cherry. 'It's maybe a little too atmospheric. Shall we go back upstairs now? There are lots of other things to see. There's a tall turret somewhere with one hundred twirly steps leading up to it.'

'Ooh!' said Jasper, 'I'd like to go up there!'

'Me too!' said Bruno.

The class began to make its way back upstairs but Dad lingered behind.

'What's in there?' he asked, pointing at a narrow door in the wall, which none of us had spotted before. 'Shall we open it?'

'Erm . . .' I began, as the last of my classmates disappeared up the dungeon steps.

'Come on,' said Dad. 'We can always catch the others up. Let's take a quick look!'

Chapter FOUR

Dad hurried across the room and pulled open the door. A cloud of dust billowed into the air and spiders scuttled across the floor. Pink Rabbit jumped in alarm. He hates spiders.

'I don't think there's anything in there, Dad,' I said as we peered into the dark space behind the door. 'I think it's

just some sort of cupboard.'

'Hmm,' said Dad,
peering closer and
brushing away the spiderwebs.
'But what's that?' He pointed up into
one corner where there was
something shadowy and
silvery all curled up.

'OH . . .' I said, staring at it in wonder. 'Is it? Is it . . . ?'

'A ghost!' said Dad. 'Yes! I think it is!'

I felt little shivers prick all the way up and down my spine. I had never seen a real ghost before, even though Dad goes on about them all the time.

Suddenly I felt a little bit afraid.

'Shut the door again, Dad,' I said. 'I don't think we should disturb it.'

'Rubbish!' said Dad as the ghost began to uncurl itself in the corner of the cupboard. 'Look—it's friendly!'

But I didn't think the ghost looked very friendly. It raised its shimmery, glimmery arms up into the air and opened its mouth into a wide 'O' shape.

'OOOooohhh!' it moaned.

I put my hands over my eyes.

'It's just pretending,' laughed Dad. 'I can do that too! OOOoooohh!!'

I peeped out from behind my fingers
and saw that the ghost was looking very
surprised.

'OOOOOoooooooOOOOOOHHHHH!'
it wailed again, but this time much more
loudly.

'OOOOOoooooooOOOOOOHHHHH!'

copied Dad.

The ghost looked
a bit cross. He crossed
his silvery arms across
his chest and frowned.

'You are supposed
to run away when

I do that,' he said.
'That's what usually
happens.'

'But why?'
asked Dad. 'I
thought we could have
a nice chat!'

'A chat?' said the ghost. 'I haven't had
one of those in years! Two hundred to be
exact.'

Dad looked horrified. 'Two hundred
years!' he exclaimed. 'You mean to say
you haven't spoken to anyone in TWO
HUNDRED YEARS?!'

The ghost hung his head sadly.

'You must have been very lonely,' continued Dad. 'Very lonely indeed.'

'I have,' said the ghost, giving a little sniff. 'I used to try and talk to people but they always ran away screaming, so in the end I gave up. Now I just try and scare them on purpose instead. It's much easier because that's what people expect from a ghost.'

'Mmm,' nodded Dad.

'Mostly, though,' continued the ghost, 'I hide in the cupboard. I don't really like scaring people, and sometimes they throw things at me.'

'Oh dear . . .' soothed Dad. 'That can't be fun.'

'It's not,' said the ghost. 'I just wish people could see me for who I am and not what I am.'

'Indeed,' said Dad, stroking his chin thoughtfully. 'Well, I'm sure it can't be too hard to get people to see that you're friendly. Why don't you come with us? We're on a school trip and we could introduce you to the rest of the class. I'm sure none of them would be frightened of you once we explain who you are. What's your name?'

'Oscar,' said the ghost, holding out his cold, silvery hand for Dad and me to shake. I took his hand but it didn't feel solid at all. It was like shaking hands with a cloud!

'OK, Oscar,' said Dad. 'You just come with us. 'We'll introduce you to everyone!'

Oscar seemed a bit doubtful but he floated out of the cupboard and followed Dad and me across the dungeon floor. As we neared the stone steps I noticed a dressing-up box standing against the wall in the gloom.

'Wait!' I said, running over to it. 'Let's see what costumes are in this room!'

I opened the box and pulled out a black and white striped jumpsuit.

'A prisoner costume!' I said.

'Oh, that is nice,' said Dad. 'I am a fan of black and white stripes. You should put it on, Isadora. It would suit you!'

Hurriedly I pulled the jumpsuit on over my clothes. There was a papier mâché ball and chain attached to one of the ankles, which dragged along the ground when I walked.

Oscar shivered. 'I remember the days when there were real prisoners down here,' he said.

The three of us made our way back up the dungeon steps and back into the corridor above. As we walked I started to feel uneasy.

'Dad,' I said, tugging on his sleeve, 'I think the class might be frightened of Oscar if we just turn up with him like this. Maybe we should introduce him to them in a different way?'

Oscar looked a bit sad as I said this but I didn't want him to feel offended when all my friends started screaming.

'Don't be silly,' said Dad. 'Who could be scared of Oscar? He's such a friendly ghost. Look at his smiley face!

No, we'll just introduce him to the class and explain that he's our friend.'

'But—' I said.

'It will be fine, Isadora,' Dad insisted. 'Don't worry.'

Oscar seemed reassured. He even started to smile! But his smile didn't last for long. We rounded the corner and I saw Miss Cherry and my classmates all standing in a group. Miss Cherry was ticking off names on a clipboard and looking confused.

'I am sure we are missing two people and a pink rabbit . . .' she was saying.

Then she looked up and saw us.
My friends all looked up and saw us.

And they SCREAMED.

Every single one of them.

Even Miss Cherry.

'AAAARRRGGGHHHHHH!!!!'
she shouted, dropping
her clipboard on the
floor and turning
as white as a
ghost herself.
   'EEEEK!!'
shrieked
Samantha, keeling
over onto the floor in
                    fright.

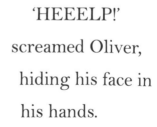

                    'HEEELP!'
            screamed Oliver,
               hiding his face in
               his hands.

'IT'S THE GHOST!!!' yelled Jasper.

Oscar, who had been floating down the corridor in front of us, jerked backwards in fright. His smile disappeared immediately.

'Wait!' said Dad, holding up his hands. 'Everyone, listen. This ghost is friendly.'

But no one listened. They all turned round and RAN.

Chapter FIVE

'Oh dear,' sighed Dad.

'I did tell you,' I said.

Oscar gave a sad little sniff and began to glide away, back towards the dungeon below.

'Hey!' I called. 'Oscar, come back!'

But Oscar didn't turn round. He floated all the way back down the corridor and towards the dungeon.

'What a shame!' said Dad as we stood together in the now empty corridor. 'Poor Oscar.'

'I did tell you!' I said again.

'You did,' sighed Dad. 'You were right, Isadora. We need to find a different way to introduce the ghost to the class.'

We made our way back along the corridor to the dungeon.

'Oscar!' I called as we hurried down the stone steps. 'Where are you?'

'Are you in here again?' asked Dad, opening the cupboard door. We both peered into the darkness. There was the little silvery shape, trembling in the corner where it had been before.

'Oscar!' I said. 'Come out! Don't be afraid!'

'But I am afraid,' sobbed Oscar. 'I'm afraid I'm never going to have any friends.'

'You will!' I insisted. 'We just have to find the right way to introduce you.'

'And you already have two friends!' added Dad. 'Me and Isadora.'

Oscar sniffed. 'That's true,' he said, cheering up a little bit. He uncurled himself and floated out of the cupboard.

'Right,' said Dad. 'We need to think of something quickly. Before the end of the school trip!'

'Yes!' I agreed. 'We need to think of some way that Oscar can join in without anyone noticing that he is a ghost.'

'Hmm . . .' said Dad.

Pink Rabbit started to twitch his ears and tug at my prisoner costume. I looked down at my stripy legs and at the ball and chain attached to my ankle.

'I wonder . . .' I began. 'I wonder if there are any costumes in the castle that Oscar would be able to wear. If we could find one with a hood then it would hide his face and no one would be able to tell he was a ghost.'

'What a good idea!' said Dad.

Oscar started to jiggle up and down in the air excitedly. 'I know where all the costumes are in the castle!' he said. 'I have been living here for two hundred years after all! I know there's a monk costume with a hood in the chapel, but—even better—there's another knight costume in the room where all the swords and shields are. It's got a metal helmet!'

'Perfect!' said Dad. 'We need to get there fast, in case the others decide to go there before us. Come on!'

Oscar, Pink Rabbit, and I followed
Dad as he swished out of the dungeon and
back up the steps.

'I'll show you the way!' said Oscar,
whizzing ahead. We zoomed along
the corridor, back through the throne
room, and up a grand staircase to the
first floor.

We hurtled along a twisty corridor,
past lots of paintings and into a
big room that had hundreds
of shiny swords and
shields pinned to
the walls.

I spotted the dressing-up box in the corner of the room and ran to open it.

'Here it is!' I gasped, holding up a different kind of knight costume to the ones Bruno had found earlier. This one had a helmet with a big plume of feathers sticking out of it.

'Wow!' said Dad. 'That is swanky!'

Oscar floated into the costume and I put the helmet onto his head.

'You need to remember to stay on the ground,' I told him. 'No rising up into the air!'

'Yes,' agreed Dad. 'That would give the game away!'

Oscar sank to the ground.

'We need to find the others now,' I said. 'I wonder where they are.'

After searching the castle for fifteen minutes, we finally found Miss Cherry and the rest of the class in the entrance hall.

'I tell you, it was a real ghost!' Miss Cherry was saying to the man in the ticket booth. 'It chased us down the corridor!'

'It was coming to attack us!' Jasper said.

'I see,' said the man in an amused sort of way.

Then Miss Cherry turned round and saw Dad and me. Her face took on a frightened look again.

'It's OK,' said Dad. 'There's no ghost. 'Look. It's gone.'

Miss Cherry put her hand on her heart.

'Thank goodness for that!' she said. 'But who's that child in the knight costume?'

'Oh, that's Oscar,' said Dad. 'He was lost and trying to find the . . . erm . . .

lunch hall. So I said he could come
with us.'

Miss Cherry looked at her watch.

'Ah, yes, lunch,' she said. 'I think
lunch might be a good idea right now.
Follow me, everyone!'

We all followed Miss Cherry to the
lunch hall and sat down at long wooden
tables.

'That was the scariest thing I've ever
seen!' said Zoe as she sat down next to me
and opened her lunchbox.

'Same,' agreed Oliver. 'I can't believe we saw a real ghost!'

Oscar sat next to me and didn't say anything. I hoped no one would notice that he didn't have a lunchbox of his own. I handed him a sandwich under the table.

'I can't eat that!' he whispered. 'Ghosts don't eat food!'

'Oh!' I said. 'Of course! Well, maybe you should pretend to eat it anyway.'

Oscar took the sandwich and put it in front of him on the table.

'So where are you from, Oscar?' asked Zoe.

'Er . . .' began Oscar.

'Yeah, and which room did you get that knight costume from?' asked Bruno. 'It's much better than my one!'

'So much better,' agreed Sashi wistfully. 'It has a proper helmet!'

'I still haven't got a costume!' complained Samantha. 'I want to be a princess!'

'I know where the princess costume is!' said Oscar. 'It's in the royal bedroom.'

'Really?!' said Samantha excitedly.
'How do you know that? You must have
been round the whole castle already!'

'I have,' said Oscar truthfully.

'Ooh,' said Jasper. 'What other costumes are there to find, then?'

Oscar started to list all the different dressing-up outfits that were hidden round the castle.

'I want the bowman's outfit!' yelled Jasper. 'I can be like Robin Hood!'

'Quiet please, Bruno,' called Miss Cherry from the next table. 'We'll be off to the archery room after lunch.'

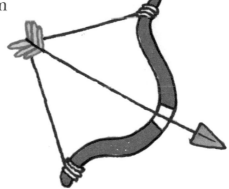

'The archery room?' asked Samantha. 'What's that?'

'It's the place where they keep all the bows and arrows,' explained Oscar. 'And there's a section where you are allowed to have a go yourself. It's really fun.'

'Ooh,' said Jasper. 'I can't wait for that.'

I stayed quiet and ate my lunch. It made me happy to see Oscar so happy. He was having such a good time telling my friends all about the castle. They all seemed very impressed.

'You do know a lot, Oscar,' said Sashi as we finished our lunches and stood up from the table. 'You must be very clever!'

'Oh,' said Oscar, looking pleased and embarrassed. 'Well . . . I just have a lot of time on my hands!'

Chapter SIX

After lunch we all followed Miss Cherry
to the archery room, including Oscar.
Jasper raced towards the dressing-up box
and pulled out the bowman's outfit.

'I'm just like Robin Hood now!' he
cried, putting it on over his clothes.

Then it was time for an archery
lesson. A lady came in and showed us how

to use a bow and arrow. We had to shoot it across the room and try and hit the target on the other side.

'It's really hard,' said Sashi as her arrow went flying up towards the high ceiling.

'Really hard!' agreed Jasper. 'Even with my bowman's outfit on!'

Oscar was the last to have a turn.

'Wow!' said everyone as Oscar's arrow hit the bullseye. 'Amazing!'

'Well done!' said the lady, sounding really impressed. 'See if you can do it again!' She handed Oscar another arrow and Oscar shot it right in the bullseye for the second time.

'Double wow!' said the lady. 'You are really talented.'

'Woahhhh!' said the class, and Jasper's eyes almost popped out of his head.

'You are awesome, Oscar!' he said.

Oscar shuffled his feet with embarrassment but I could tell he was really pleased.

'I can teach you how to do it sometime, if you like,' he offered.

Jasper nodded his head eagerly.

'Yes please!' he said.

After the archery we made our way upstairs and looked around some of the other rooms including the one full of swords and shields, and the tall turret with one hundred steps leading up to it. Samantha found the princess outfit in the royal bedroom.

'It's time for the last room!' said Miss Cherry once we were back on the ground floor again. 'It's the chapel. I expect there's one more costume left in there too. Who isn't dressed up yet?'

'Me!' said Dominic. 'I want to be a knight or a bowman!'

'Oh dear,' said Miss Cherry. 'I'm afraid it's more likely that you'll be a monk.'

The chapel was a very beautiful room with high arched ceilings and lots of carvings covered in a thin layer of silver called silver leaf. Joined on to the chapel was another fancy room with a huge complicated-looking instrument in it.

'Oh my!' said Dad. 'An organ! I would so love to be able to play the organ! Very gothic and vampire-y, don't you think?' He sat down on the seat and started to press the notes. A tuneless song came out and everyone put their fingers in their ears.

'Dad,' I hissed. 'I don't think you're supposed to touch that!'

'It's quite all right,' said an official-looking man who was standing nearby. 'We encourage people to have a go on the instruments. In fact,' he said, gesturing

towards the table next to him, 'there
are lots of medieval instruments for the
children to try out just here!' He picked up
one of them and handed it to Oliver.

'This is a lute,' he said. 'Have a go.'

Oliver started to twang on the lute

as the man handed out the rest of the instruments to the class. There was a horn, a flute, a tambourine, a harp, a wooden recorder as well as several others.

'I know how to play the recorder!' said Zoe.

'I want to play the tambourine!' said Sashi.

'Can I try the harp?' asked Samantha shyly.

Soon everyone in the class had an instrument to play. There was an almighty racket as Oliver strummed his lute, Sashi banged her tambourine, Samantha plucked at her harp, Dominic blew on the flute, Zoe puffed on the recorder, Bruno honked on a trumpet, Jasper banged on a drum, I tootled on the horn, and Oscar played on the organ.

'This is so much fun!' shouted Bruno. 'It's like we're in a band!'

'It is!' yelled Sashi. 'We should start a

band and have band practice every week!'

'That would be so great!' cried Zoe. 'We could put on a concert.'

'I think you might all need a bit more practice before then,' bellowed Dad, putting his fingers in his ears.

But there was one 'person' who didn't seem to need any practice. Over the sound of all the squeaking, squawking, crashing instruments was the sound of the organ. And it was being played beautifully. A haunting, bewitching melody rang out over the noise as Oscar ran his silvery fingers up and down the notes. One by one my friends all stopped playing their instruments and began to listen to the angelic sound of the organ.

'That is such a pretty tune!' sighed Samantha as she put down her harp.

'Amazing,' said Sashi.

'We definitely need Oscar for our band,' said Bruno.

'Definitely,' agreed Jasper.

Miss Cherry, who had closed her eyes to listen to the music suddenly frowned and looked up.

'Who's Oscar?' she said.

Oscar's fingers stopped moving over the notes of the organ and came to rest slowly in his lap. He didn't say anything.

'Hang on . . .' said Miss Cherry, counting all the children in the room. 'This boy is not part of the class!' She narrowed her eyes at Dad. 'Didn't you say you were taking him to the lunch hall?'

'Er . . .' said Dad.

Miss Cherry started to look panicked.

'We must find his parents!' she

wailed. 'Or we might be accused of kidnap!'

'We won't be accused of kidnap,' said Dad. 'Oscar doesn't have any parents.'

Miss Cherry looked confused and Oscar hung his head sadly.

'It's true,' he said. 'I don't have anyone.'

'What do you mean?' asked Miss Cherry in bewilderment. 'Everyone has someone.'

'Not Oscar,' I said, going over to where he was sitting at the organ and putting my hand on his shoulder. Miss Cherry, Dad, and the class all stared up at us.

'There's something special about Oscar,' I said. 'He's . . . he's . . .'

'He's what?' asked Sashi.

'Tell us!' said Bruno.

'Ooh, is it a secret?' asked Zoe.

'Well, yes . . .' I said. 'Sort of.

You have to promise not to scream
or run away.'

'Of course we won't run away!'
scoffed Bruno. 'Oscar is awesome!'

'Yes!' agreed Zoe. 'We love Oscar!
What could possibly be scary about him?'

'Exactly!' I said. 'Nothing at all!'

Carefully I lifted the helmet from
Oscar's head and put it on the floor.

My friends and Miss Cherry all gasped.

'Is that . . . is that . . . ?' they stuttered.

'It's the ghost we saw earlier,' I explained. 'But he's not scary, he's really nice. He just wants to make friends.'

Bruno took a deep breath and stepped forwards.

'I would love to be your friend, Oscar,' he said. 'I'm sorry I was frightened of you before.'

'I'm sorry too,' said Zoe. 'I should have got to know you before I decided to run away.'

'Me too,' agreed Sashi.

One by one my friends all stepped

forward to shake Oscar's silvery hand.
Oscar beamed from ear to ear and I could
tell he was really happy.

'It's been lovely to meet you, Oscar,'
said Miss Cherry, taking her turn to shake
his hand. 'Definitely an experience I'm
sure none of us will forget!' She looked

down at her watch and made a small tutting sound.

'Oh dear,' she said. 'We are running a bit late for the coach. I am afraid it's time to go home. You had better all take off your costumes.'

'Oh no!' said Zoe.

'I don't want to go back yet,' said Bruno.

'But what about Oscar?' asked Sashi. 'We need him for our band!'

Oscar sat on the stool by the organ and hung his head. He seemed very sad again now.

'I wish I could be in your band,' he said. 'Today has been the best day I've had in a very long time! I hope you will all visit again. It gets very lonely in this castle.'

'I can only imagine,' said Dad glumly.

I thought of our lovely warm home, with Mum and Baby Honeyblossom and Pink Rabbit. I looked at Dad, and knew we were thinking the same thing.

'I know,' he said. 'Why don't you

come back with us? You can come and live in our vampire fairy house. What do you think?'

'Oh yes!' I exclaimed. 'We have a very nice attic with lots of nooks and crannies!'

'In fact, we are in need of a house ghost. All the best vampires have them,' said Dad.

'Really?!' said Oscar. 'You would really let me come and haunt your house?'

'Of course!' said Dad. 'We are a ghost-friendly family.'

Oscar smiled the biggest smile I had ever seen in my life and the whole class cheered.

'That would be amazing,' he said. 'I would love that. It would be the best thing to happen to me in two hundred years!'

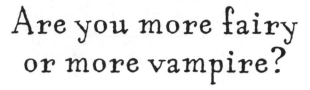

Are you more fairy or more vampire?

Take the quiz to find out!

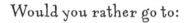

What's your favourite colour?

A. Pink   **B.** Black   **C.** I love them both!

Would you rather go to:

A. A glittery school that teaches magic, ballet, and making flowery crowns?

B. A spooky school that teaches gliding, bat training, and how to have the sleekest hair possible?

C. A school where everyone gets to be totally different and interesting?

On your camping holiday, do you:

A. Put up your tent with a wave of your magic wand and go exploring?

B. Pop up your fold-out four-poster bed and avoid the sun?

C. Splash about in the sea and have a great time?

Results

Mostly As

You are a glittery, dancing fairy and you love nature!

Mostly Bs

You are a sleek, caped vampire and you love the night!

Mostly Cs

You are half fairy, half vampire and totally unique — just like Isadora Moon!

Isadora Moon

Isadora Moon
Goes to School

Her mum is a fairy and her dad is a vampire
and she is a bit of both. She loves the night, bats,
and her black tutu, but she also loves the sunshine,
her magic wand, and Pink Rabbit.

When it's time for Isadora to start school
she's not sure where she belongs—fairy school
or vampire school?

Isadora Moon
Goes Camping

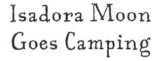

It is the first day back at school after the summer, and Isadora is called on to talk about her holidays at show-and-tell. She's worried. She had been to the seaside, like her friends, but strange things had happened there . . . the sort of things that probably didn't happen on human holidays.

Isadora Moon
Gets in Trouble

Isadora wants to take Pink Rabbit in to Bring
Your Pet to School Day, but her older cousin Mirabelle
has a much better plan—why not take a dragon?

What could possibly go wrong...?

Harriet Muncaster

Harriet Muncaster, that's me! I'm the
author and illustrator of Isadora Moon.
Yes really! I love anything teeny tiny,
anything starry, and everything glittery.

Love Isadora Moon?
Why not try these too...